Don't Let Go!

For Sophie,
Joan and Geoff – J.W.

Text copyright © 2002 by Jeanne Willis. Illustrations copyright © 2002 by Tony Ross.
The rights of Jeanne Willis and Tony Ross to be identified as the author and illustrator of this work
have been asserted by them in accordance with the Copyright, Designs and Patents Act, 1988.

First published in Great Britain in 2002 by Andersen Press Ltd., 20 Vauxhall Bridge Road, London SW1V 2SA.
Published in Australia by Random House Australia Pty., 20 Alfred Street, Milsons Point, Sydney, NSW 2061.
All rights reserved. Colour separated in Switzerland by Photolitho AG, Zürich.
Printed and bound in Italy by Grafiche AZ, Verona.

10   9   8   7   6   5   4   3   2   1

British Library Cataloguing in Publication Data available.

ISBN 1 84270 071 5

This book has been printed on acid-free paper

Don't Let Go!

Jeanne Willis and Tony Ross

Andersen Press
London

"Teach me to ride and I'll ride to you,
I could ride from ours to yours.
Please will you, Daddy? I need to learn,

And Mum is too busy indoors.

I tried in the yard but it's ever so hard;
I bloodied my knee on the wall.

The road is too rough, I'm not clever enough –
And my bike is too fast and I'll fall."

"Wherever you go, there are slippery slopes
And ups and downs and bumps.
There will always be difficult paths to take
And giant steps and humps . . .

But the view when you get to the top of the hill
And the feel of the wind in your hair . . .

And the freedom to go wherever you please
And to know you can get yourself there,
That must be worth a few little knocks
And the odd little bruise or two.

But if you're not ready, we'll wait a while –
Whatever you want to do."

"I'll try in a minute – at least, I might.
I'm getting myself prepared,
Checking my helmet and bicycle bell –

But, Daddy, I'm really scared!"
"Sophie, I'm here – I won't let go,
Not until you say . . .

Hold on tight. I love you, so
We'll do this together, OK?"

"I think I'm ready to go now, Dad.
Daddy, don't let go!
Don't let go . . .
you can let go . . ."

. . . NOW!

Bye, Daddeeee . . .
you're so slow!

Look at me, Daddy! I can ride!
See? I can ride my bike . . .
Now I can go wherever I please –
To the end of the world if I like!"

"It's awfully difficult letting go,
I was scared too, today —

*Scared you would never come back to me
Now you can ride away.*"

"Daddy, I'm here, I won't let go.
Not until you say.
Hold on tight. I love you, so –
We'll do this together . . .

. . . OK?"